It's a Tea Party!

Grosset & Dunlap

To my sister, Minoli, with love—S.F.

To my wonderful girlfriends—E.H.

Special thanks to Heidi Marotta and Willie Bourne.

Library of Congress Cataloging-in-Publication Data is available.

ISBN 0-448-42162-3   A B C D E F G H I J

It's a Tea Party!

By Sonali Fry

Photographs by
Elizabeth Hathon

Grosset & Dunlap, Publishers

Janell has invited Carly,
Nicole, and Gabrielle over to
her house. They are sitting
outside, trying to think of
something to do.

"It's such a beautiful day,"
says Janell. "Why don't we
have a tea party?"

They walk around in the yard and find the perfect spot!

It's not too sunny, and not too shady. Also, there's a table already there.

The girls are very excited! They hurry back to the house
to prepare for the party.

Carly and Janell make invitations.

They use markers, crayons, and pretty stamp pads to decorate them.

When they're done, they put them in envelopes. Now it's time to deliver them!

Together, the girls deliver the invitations to all their friends.

Back at home, the girls bake some cupcakes.
Oops! Baking can be messy, but it sure is fun!

Soon all the goodies are ready!

Next, while Nicole picks some flowers for the center of the table...

…Janell's mom shows Janell and Carly how to fold napkins into pretty shapes.

Now it's time to get dressed!
The girls find fancy clothes to wear.
Look—Nicole has found a pretty pink dress!

They also fix their hair and put on some makeup.

Don't they look great?

Okay, it's time to get this show on the road!

First, the girls put a pretty white tablecloth on the table. Then, they arrange the food, china, and napkins. They fill the teapot with apple juice. Everything looks so nice!

"Jillian and Catherine are here," says Nicole.

Two guests have arrived!

The girls sit down. The teddy bears join the party, too!
Janell pours "tea" for everyone.
Let the party begin!

"Try one of our yummy cupcakes," says Carly.

Bottoms up! Soon, it's time for seconds.

Now it's Gillian's turn to pour.

The teddy bears are thirsty, too!

Look—it's Jake and Wyatt. Now everyone has arrived!

"Nice hat," says Jake to Janell.

"Thanks," says Janell.

"Would you gentlemen like some tea?" asks Gabrielle.

Everyone has fun talking, eating, and laughing.

"Hey, my cup is empty!" yells Jake. "It looks like you need a refill," says Gabrielle.

Isn't she a great hostess?

Afterward, everyone is ready to play croquet. First, they need to clear the table. They carefully place the food, juice, and china next to a tree.

Wyatt quickly takes one more sip of "tea."

They get out the croquet equipment...

...and set up the court.

Ready, set, let's play croquet!

"Great shot, Janell," says Catherine.

"Way to go, Gillian!" says Nicole.
    What a fun game!

As evening comes, the guests start to go home.

"Thank you for coming to our tea party," say the girls, as they wave good-bye. "We hope you had a good time!"

The hosts and their guests really enjoyed themselves. Did *you*?